MW00815386

The Ghost in the Classroom

The Ghost
in the Classroom

By Gerda Wagener
Illustrated by Uli Waas

Translated by J. Alison James

North-South Books
NEW YORK • LONDON

First published in the United States, Great Britain, Canada,
Australia, and New Zealand in 1997 by North-South Books,
an imprint of Nord-Süd Verlag AG, Gossau Zürich, Switzerland.

Distributed in the United States by North-South Books Inc., New York.

Library of Congress Cataloging-in-Publication Data is available.
ISBN 1-55858-799-3 (TRADE BINDING)
ISBN 1-55858-800-0 (LIBRARY BINDING)

A CIP catalogue record for this book
is available from The British Library.

1 3 5 7 9 TB 10 8 6 4 2
1 3 5 7 9 LB 10 8 6 4 2
Printed in Belgium

Tina lived alone with her mother and
father. She had no sisters and no brothers
and no dog and no fish and no cat.

Tina didn't want a brother or a sister.
Tina didn't want a dog or a fish.

She wanted a cat.

Tina went to school.

Her teacher was very nice.

She let all the children do a project.
They could do a project on anything
they liked.

Tina did a project on cats. All the time
she studied, she thought about the cat
that she wanted.

Tina sat next to Anthony. Anthony was Tina's best friend, and Anthony could draw cats.

Anthony drew a cat for Tina's project. It was a beautiful picture of a cat.

But what was a picture compared to a real cat? Tina sighed.

She asked her parents once again.

"But Tina," said her mother.

"But Tina," said her father.

"You need time to take care of a pet," said Mother.

"And time is something we don't have," said Dad. "Subject closed."

What could Tina say to that?

And then one day a strange thing
happened.

During lunch Tina made a discovery:
Otto! Otto was hiding in Tina's lunch
box.

Otto was small. Very, very small. Otto was a ghost. A small white ghost. On Tina's sandwich.

"Yuck!" squealed Otto. "How revolting. Jam. I hate jam. My shirt already stinks of jam. Get me out of here!"

Otto hopped over the edge of the box. He started to run away.

"Wait," cried Tina. "Wait a second."

"I'm out of here," said Otto. "Away from that stinky jam."

"But what if Miss Wheeler sees you?" said Tina.

"No problem," said Otto. "I'm invisible to grown-ups."

"Only children can see you?" asked Tina.

"Exactly," said Otto. "After all, I am a
school ghost. I used to be a castle ghost.
In a royal castle! Then only princes and
princesses could see me."

"Wow," said Tina.

"But these days there is more happening in schools than in castles, if you know what I mean."

Tina didn't, but she nodded anyway.

"And now, time for a little spooking,"
cried Otto, and he rubbed his hands
together.

"No!" said Tina. "It's time for class to
start." She tried to grab Otto, but he
slipped right through her fingers.

Miss Wheeler came into the class.
All the children sat in their seats.
"It's more fun to spook during class
time," Otto whispered loudly. He balanced
on Anthony's ruler.

Tina tried to catch Otto again.

But instead, she knocked the ruler to
the floor. Otto gave the ruler a swift kick.
It slid under Miss Wheeler's desk.

"Goodness, Tina!" said Miss Wheeler.

Otto flew around the class like a big fat white bee.

Otto popped off
his head and tucked
it under his arm.
That looked really disgusting! Then he
played catch with his head. "Ooo-up
you go!" he said, and "Wheeeee!"
he giggled coming down.

Anthony clapped with
delight, and Tina was
enchanted.

Miss Wheeler
wanted to have
a reading lesson.
But Otto banged the
reading books shut,
one by one. BAM!
BAM! BAM!

Then BAMMM! he
banged Miss Wheeler's
book shut and it fell
to the floor.

Miss Wheeler looked at Tina.

"It wasn't me," said Tina.

"I see. Then it must have been a ghost."

"Exactly," said Tina. She had to giggle.

"Giggle, giggle, belly wiggle!" cried Otto.

He swooped around and tickled the
children with his ghostly fingers. Soon all
the children were giggling and laughing
just like Tina.

"Quiet, children, QUIET!" shouted Miss
Wheeler. But the children could not calm
down.

Now Otto was in full swing. He grabbed
things off the desks and flung them across
the room. Soon everyone joined in.

It was a wild rumpus, and Tina and
Anthony were right in the middle.

Miss Wheeler started to laugh. "I
suppose that's the end of our reading
lesson for today," she said.

Otto thought of something new. He
dangled from the cupboard. "Peeyooo! It
stinks up here," he shrieked. "It smells
clean. Disgustingly clean!"

Otto pulled out some sticky green slime
from his pocket. At once the class smelled
dank and musty, like the dungeon of a
haunted castle.

"Oooh, yes!" cried Otto. "What sublime
slime!" He let some dribble down onto
Miss Wheeler's desk.

"Oh, my!" said Miss Wheeler. "This
classroom really is haunted!"

"It's Otto," called Anthony. "He is
sitting on the cupboard."

But Miss Wheeler couldn't see Otto.
She asked Anthony to draw a picture of
Otto on the board.

"I can't draw ghosts," Anthony said.
"Just cats." Anthony drew her a cat.

When he saw the cat, Otto turned
himself into a ghost dog. He had a long
blue tongue and glowing red eyes.

The children shrieked.

"Does everyone remember the ghost song?" asked Miss Wheeler. "Why don't we sing it for Otto."

"Oh, yes!" cried all the children. "Let's sing the ghost song!"

Swift as lightning, Otto turned himself back into a ghost.

Otto was proud that the children were going to sing for him. He took two bones from his pocket. He beat them in time to the song.

When school was over, Otto insisted on going home with Tina. Why not? thought Tina. He is invisible to Mother and Dad anyway.

"But you have to promise to behave yourself," she said.

"I promise," said Otto. "I will behave myself."

"Are you sure?" asked Tina.

"Cross my eyes and hope to die!"

Otto sat on Tina's shoulder. "Aren't ghosts already dead?" Tina asked. But Otto didn't answer.

At home Otto rang the bell over and over. DING, DONG! DING, DONG!

"That wasn't me," said Tina, when her mother opened the door. "It was a ghost."

Mother didn't scold her, but she thought that Tina was telling stories. She couldn't see Otto, of course.

Otto played one prank after another.
He knocked books down from the
shelves. He swung on the light. He
whistled through all the keyholes, and
the keys fell clattering to the floor.

Otto filled the sugar bowl with salt.
Mama's coffee tasted terrible.

"Oh, Tina!" cried Mother. "What is
going on with you today?"

"It wasn't me, honestly!" said Tina. "It
was a ghost from school. His name is Otto."

Tina glared at Otto. "You promised
you'd behave yourself!" she whispered
loudly.

"I am. I'm behaving terribly!" cried Otto.

In the kitchen Otto almost fell into the
honey jar. Of course, honey spilled
everywhere.

"Tina!" said Mother. "That is enough."

"Mother," said Tina, "I am telling you the truth. Ask Miss Wheeler."

"I believe something happened at school today," said her mother, and she picked up the phone.

While she was talking, Otto took out three plump black spiders from his pocket and told them to go and make webs.

Mother hung up the phone and shook her head in amazement. "It must be true. A small, invisible ghost?"

"Named Otto," said Tina.

Later Otto made a complete mess out of Tina's notebook.

"I wonder if I could suck him up in the vacuum cleaner," her mother said. "Along with his spiderwebs."

"Not on your life!" bellowed Otto.

He spread itching powder on Mother's chair. "I will never, ever go. I am your sweet little ghostie-o."

Dad couldn't believe that there was a ghost in the house. He had to see Otto for himself. "Even if he is tiny," said Dad, "he must be visible."

First Dad got the binoculars.

Then he got the magnifying glass.

Finally he tried to take a photo of Otto.
But Otto was invisible even in the picture.
Of course.

Dad didn't understand ghosts at all,
thought Tina.

Otto laughed. "That man is a real
nincompoop!" he said, and then he slid
some ice cubes down the back of Dad's
shirt.

Dad lost his temper. He jumped up and
stormed out of the house.

When Dad came home, he had a thick
book from the library. It was called *All
About Ghosts*. He bent over it, reading.

"Here," he cried finally. "'How to Get
Rid of a Small Ghost.' Page 416."

Tina read what her father showed her:
"A cat in the house drives away
troublesome rodent-sized ghosts."

"A cat!" whispered Tina.

This time the whole family went out.
Otto stayed behind.

They went straight to the animal shelter.

There were so many wonderful cats that Tina had a hard time choosing just one. But finally she decided on a big black cat with a white face and white paws.

When they got home, Tina hugged her parents. "Oh, thank you!" she said. "I promise I'll look after the cat myself."

"Well," said her mother, "maybe we can help a bit."

"Of course!" said her father. "Now let's see if this book about ghosts was right."

"Come here, Otto," called Tina. Otto trembled in fear.

"I got you a cat, but don't expect me to like it!" said Otto.

Tina stared at Otto. Very hard. "Is this all your doing?" she asked.

Otto winked at Tina. "I hate to boast," he said, "but I am a ghost. Wasn't it clever the way I got your parents to let you have a cat?"

"It was . . . magic!" said Tina. She grinned at Otto.

Otto grinned back. "Just one of my special tricks," he said. "Tomorrow I'm going back to school. I'm sure there are other children who could use my help."

"I think you're right," said Tina. "And there are enough cats at the shelter for every one of them."

About the Author

Gerda Wagener was born in Sauerland, a pretty, mountainous area of Germany.

She studied sociology and German language and literature, and worked first as a private tutor and then as a social worker. She now lives in Wuppertal, Germany, and has a black cat named Makki. Her first easy-to-read book for North-South, *A Mouse in the House!*, was also illustrated by Uli Waas.

About the Illustrator

Uli Waas was born in Donauworth, Bavaria. She studied painting and graphic design at the Academy of Art in Munich. She has illustrated a number of books for children, including three other easy-to-read books for North-South: *Where's Molly?*, *Spiny*, and *A Mouse in the House!* She lives with her husband and their daughter and son on the edge of the Swabian Alps.